المشي في الغابة

Walking through the Jungle

Mantra Lingua
Global House
303 Ballards Lane
London N12 8NP
www.mantralingua.com

First published in Great Britain in 1997 by Barefoot Books Ltd
First dual language edition published in 2001 by Mantra Lingua
This edition published in 2017

Printed in Paola, Malta MP280217PB03178119

المشي في الغابة
Walking through the Jungle

Illustrated by Debbie Harter

Arabic translation by Dr Sajida Fawzi

المشي في الغابة

Walking through the jungle,

ماذا ترى؟

What do you see?

I think I see a lion, chasing after me.

Roar!

زئير!

أظن أنني أرى أسداً،

يطاردني.

الطفو فوق المحيط

Floating on the ocean,

ماذا ترى؟

What do you see?

I think I see a whale, chasing after me.

Whoosh!

وروش !

أظن أنني أرى حوتاً،
يطاردني.

تسلق الجبال

Climbing in the mountains,

ماذا ترى؟

What do you see?

أظن أنني أرى ذئباً،
يطاردني.

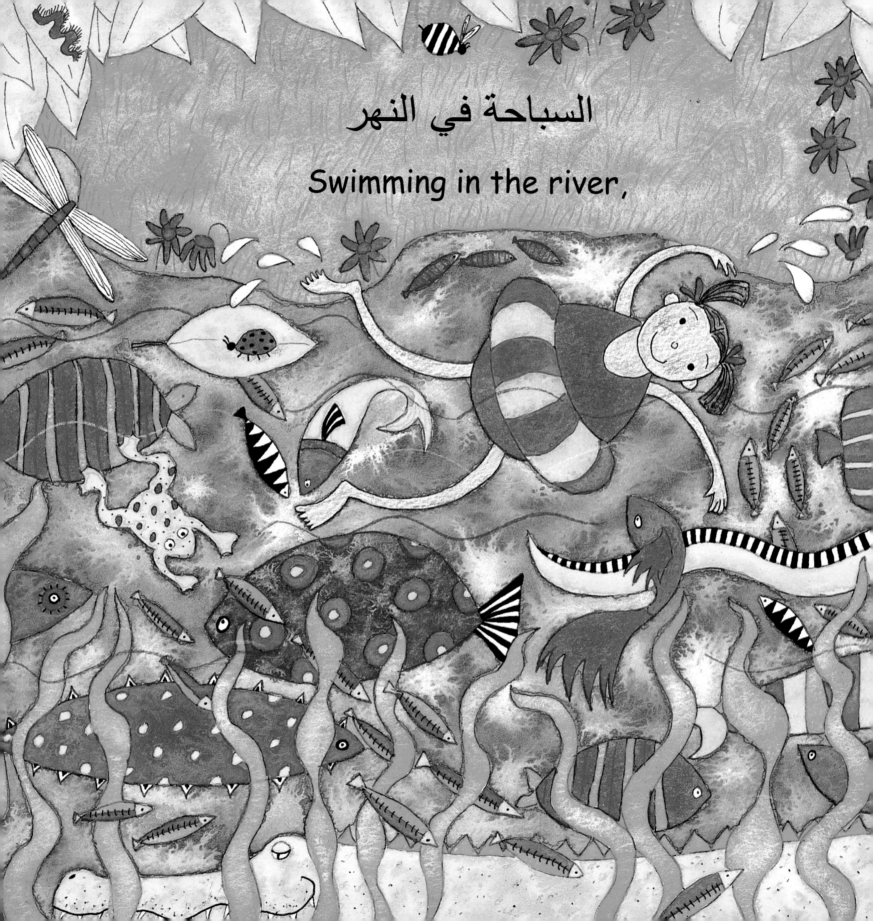

السباحة في النهر

Swimming in the river,

ماذا ترى؟

What do you see?

أظن أنني أرى تمساحاً،
يطارني.

التجول في الصحراء

Trekking in the desert,

ماذا ترى؟

What do you see?

أظن أنني أرى ثعباناً،
يطاردني.

التزحلق على جبل الثلج

Slipping on the iceberg,

ماذا ترى؟

What do you see?

I think I see a polar bear,
chasing after me.

Growl!

عواء !

أظن أنني أرى دباً قطبياً،
يطاردني.

الجري إلى البيت للعشاء

Running home for supper,

أين كنت؟

Where have you been?

درتُ حول العالم ورجعت،

I've been around the world and back,

فاحزر ماذا رأيت؟

And guess what I have seen?